Lalaloopsy

Sew Magical! Sew Cute!

Harmony Takes the Stage

by Lauren Cecil

SCHOLASTIC INC.

ISBN 978-0-545-53180-1

12 11 10 9 8 7 6 5 4 3 2 1   13 14 15 16 17 18/0

Printed in the U.S.A.

40

First printing, May 2013

It was a sunny day in Lalaloopsy Land. Spot Splatter Splash was outside painting.

"Hi, Spot! What are you working on?" Crumbs Sugar Cookie asked.

"A painting for our new neighbor," Spot replied. "She's moving in today. I thought she might like a present."

"A new neighbor!" Crumbs said. "How exciting! What's she like?"

"I haven't met her yet," Spot explained. "But I really hope she likes art. Then I'll have someone new to paint with."

"And I hope she likes cookies," Crumbs replied, "because I'm going to make her a special welcome-to-the-neighborhood treat!"

Crumbs rushed home to make a batch of her extra-special sugar-and-spice cookies.

Crumbs had just finished baking her cookies when her friends Bea Spells-a-Lot and Peanut Big Top dropped by.

"Want a taste?" offered Crumbs. "They're for our new neighbor."

"We're getting a new neighbor?" Bea and Peanut asked eagerly.

6

"Yes!" Crumbs replied. "I hope she likes baking as much as I do. I can't wait to swap recipes with her!"

"I hope she's funny, like I am," added Peanut. "Then we could put on a comedy show together!"

"And I hope she likes to read," says Bea. "Then we could start a book club!"

Bea was leaving her house that afternoon when she bumped into Mittens Fluff 'N' Stuff and Dot Starlight.

"Hi, Bea," Mittens said. "Where are you going with that book?"

"It's for our new neighbor," Bea replied. "We're starting a book club together."

"How wonderful!" cried Mittens. "I hope our new neighbor likes wintertime. Then we could go sledding together."

"And I hope she likes science," said Dot. "Then we could do some stargazing."

"There's only one way to find out what she likes," suggested Bea. "Let's go meet her. But first, let's round up all our friends!"

Everyone stood in front of their new neighbor's house, waiting to finally meet her.

"Is everyone ready?" Bea asked her friends.

"**I**'m a little nervous," Crumbs admitted. "What if she doesn't like baking. . . ?"

"Or stargazing," said Dot.

"Or telling jokes," added Peanut.

"Even if she doesn't like those things, she'll probably still be nice," said Spot.

Then Spot rang the doorbell.

DING-DONG!

Everyone waited to see who would answer.

"**H**i!" everyone cried when the door flew open. "Welcome to the neighborhood!"

"Hello!" said the new neighbor. "My name is Harmony B. Sharp. It's so nice to meet all of you."

"I thought you might like art, so I brought you a painting," said Spot.

"And I thought you might like sweets, so I made you some cookies," said Crumbs.

"And I thought you might like to read, so I brought you a book," added Bea.

"**A**nd I thought maybe we could put on a comedy show sometime," said Peanut.

"Or go stargazing," added Dot.

"Or go sledding together!" said Mittens.

"Thank you for the warm welcome," said Harmony. "I do like art, sweets, and books—and jokes, stargazing, and sledding. . . . But do you know what I like best of all?"

Everyone shook their heads. They couldn't wait to find out.

"**S**inging, dancing, and acting," Harmony said. "I'm a performer! Do you want to see my stage?"

"Yeah!" everyone cried.

"Here it is!" Harmony announced. "This is where the magic happens."

"Wow!" said Crumbs. "This is so great. I've never been onstage before."

"If you want, I can teach you how to sing and dance," Harmony suggested. She handed Dot a microphone.

"That sounds fun!" Dot said. "We love learning new things."

Harmony showed her new friends a song-and-dance routine she'd been working on.

Soon, all the girls were dancing, singing, and having a great time together.

Show Tonight!

"Wow, Harmony," said Mittens. "It sure is fun to be onstage."

"We're having so much fun," added Bea.

"Thanks for teaching us your dance moves," Peanut agreed. "I could do this all the time!"

"**Y**ou're all welcome to come over anytime!" Harmony said. "I love having company."

"Really?" asked Spot.

"Of course. That's what neighbors are for!" said Harmony.

Harmony invited her new friends to stay for cookies and lemonade.

"You know," Spot began, "at first I hoped that you would be just like me. But now I'm glad you're not. Everybody is different, and that's what makes each of us special!"